KU-303-730

This book belongs to:

_____

_____

_____

First published 1999 by Walker Books Ltd

87 Vauxhall Walk, London SE11 5HJ

6 8 10 9 7 5

© 1999 Lucy Cousins

Maisy™. Maisy is a registered trademark of Walker Books Ltd, London.

Based on the Audio Visual Series "Maisy". A King Rollo Films Production for
Universal Pictures Visual Programming. Original Script by Andrew Brenner.

This book has been typeset in Lucy Cousins typeface

Printed in China

British Library Cataloguing in Publication Data:
a catalogue record for this book is
available from the British Library

0-7445-6765-3 (hb)
0-7445-7216-9 (pb)

Maisy Dresses Up

Lucy Cousins

WALKER BOOKS

AND SUBSIDIARIES

LONDON • BOSTON • SYDNEY

Maisy has an invitation to Tallulah's fancy dress party.

What can she dress up as?

She looks in her dressing up box.

She could be a pirate – but Charley is dressed up as a pirate.

She could be
a queen – but
Eddie is dressed
up as a king!

She could be a firefighter – but Cyril is dressed up as a firefighter!

Maisy has a good idea! She will make a special costume.

Everyone else is already at Tallulah's house.

Then the doorbell rings and in comes... a zebra!

Oh, it's Maisy!

Hello, everyone.
It's party time.

If you're crazy for Maisy, you'll love these other books featuring Maisy and her friends.

Other titles
Maisy's ABC • Maisy Goes to Bed • Maisy Goes to the Playground

Maisy Goes Swimming • Maisy Goes to Playschool

Maisy's House • Happy Birthday, Maisy • Maisy at the Farm